END-OF-YEAR PRODUCTION

Miss Tompkins, Billy's year five form teacher, passed around a pile of books — play scripts. "Please, take a copy … quickly and quietly. "She watched until each child had one. "Now, turn to page two and read the section headed *Director's Overview*." Miss Tompkins stared at the class over the top of her glasses; she appeared severe and rather scary. As each child noticed, they fell silent and read. Nobody liked being called out for talking or not doing their work.

"Miss … " Khalid said.

"Khalid, how many more times; no shouting out. Put your hand up first." She scowled.

"Sorry, Miss." He pretended to zip his lips before raising his hand.

"Yes, Khalid, what's your question?"

"Why are we reading this?" Khalid waved around his copy of the script.

"Good question. Can anyone help him?" Miss gazed at her class. Three hands went up, including Tom's. "So, Tom, what do you think?"

"For our year-end production." Tom sat back in his chair, folded his arms across his chest, and beamed a smile.

Tom shared a table with his two best mates Billy and Ant.

"We all knew that." Ant spoke around the back of his hand so that Miss would not hear.

Miss Tompkins spoke, "We have eight weeks until you finish in year five and move into the last year at this school, and by tradition, we will entertain the whole school with a play. This year, we shall perform The Keymaster by Nick Perrin. From reading the overview, you should know that it's about time travel, going back in history, to 1066 and other important dates." Miss Tompkins saw a hand go up. "Yes, Billy."

"But, Miss, it's a musical with singing and stuff. That'll be hard." Billy looked to Ant and Tom for support. They both nodded.

"Well, Billy, you are near the end of your time in year five, as are you all, and from my experience, I think you'll do a great job, possibly the best by a year five class." Miss Tompkins stood and walked around to the front of her desk. "We need to cast; that means choose who will play which part. We also need scenery painting, costumes sewing, and props making. This production will involve the whole class, and for the main characters, rehearsals will happen late afternoon, once school has finished."

A buzz of excitement came from the children, and Khalid burst into song, "Doe, ray, me fa, so, la, ti, doeeeeee." He held the last note for as long as he could.

"Okay, Khalid." Miss Tompkins clapped

her hands, "You will have plenty of time for that. For the rest of this lesson and homework, I would like you to read the whole script and decide who you would like to be. If several people want the same part, like the Keymaster or one of the other four leading roles, we will need to hold auditions, or I will have to choose."

Billy, Ant, and Tom rode their bikes home after school, chatting all the time about the end-of-year play.

"Yeah, but I'm the creative one," Ant boasted. "Miss always says so. Remember how I won the prize for the advert project at the end of the last term." Ant pushed out his chest. "It should be me who plays the Keymaster." He looked to Billy and Tom, expecting to see them agree.

"But the Keymaster is meant to be a teacher who turns into a time traveller," Tom said. He sat upright on his bike to show how grown up he was. Speaking in his best gruff dad's voice, "So, I should play that part. I'm the tallest and look more like a grown-up."

"Maybe," Billy said. "But Khalid has a good singing voice. You heard him in class doing his doe, ray, mi thing."

"True, but when Khalid speaks, he looks down a lot, and Miss won't like that," Ant said. "When you're on stage, you have to look out at the audience and speak slowly and clearly." Ant spoke slowly and clearly to emphasise what he meant.

The three boys stopped at the road

crossing; the red man showed. Ant pressed the button.

"You need to get off and push your bike," Ant called—he could see two mums with pushchairs waiting to cross from the other side.

The red man changed to green, and the familiar beep, beep, beep sound signalled it was safe to go. "Come on, you two." Ant set off toward the far side. Only after he had crossed did he notice that Billy and Tom hadn't followed him.

"Oi, you two, get a move on," Ant called back to them.

For Billy and Tom, it proved too late; the green man had changed back to red, and the traffic started moving. Ant watched and tried to speak to them, but the car noise made it impossible.

"So, what do you think?" Billy asked Tom. "Should the Keymaster be Ant or Khalid?"

"I've not heard Ant sing. I don't know if he can." Tom still thought he should get cast as Keymaster. "Ant is good at telling jokes," Tom said. He didn't want to say anything bad about Ant since they were mates, but neither did he want to help him get the part.

The beep, beep, beep sound of the crossing made Billy and Tom look up. They saw Ant across the road, waving his arms like a windmill in a storm.

"Yeah, we're coming," Billy called to him. He turned to Tom and said, "Say nothing to Ant. I want to read the play again to decide what I'll do, but I know I'm all right with a hammer, nails, and a paint brush; maybe I'll just build scenery."

"What? Build scenery? You should go on stage, get a speaking part—"

Billy interrupted Tom, "Singing, don't you mean?"

"Okay, a singing part, but whatever, you should act. Miss will expect you to." Tom patted Billy on the back. "You wait."

"Yeah, but I'll be no good." Billy slumped his shoulders and looked at the ground as he spoke; he didn't want Ant or Tom to see his face. Billy felt awkward, swallowed up by embarrassment.

Because he'd looked down, Billy missed the surprised expression on Tom's face.

"You're nuts, Billy Field. You're one of

the best in class."

Billy didn't share Tom's confidence in himself. *Yeah, but what do you know?* He thought.

As usual, Billy and Ant cycled the rest of the way home together. They arrived outside Ant's house. Although Billy lived two streets away from Ant, after school, Billy went to his grandad's to wait for his mum to get home from work. His grandad lived just two houses away from Ant.

"See ya, mate." Ant waved goodbye to Billy and then disappeared into his garden. Ant had spotted his mum and younger sister, Max, at the rabbit hutch. Max, still grounded, had to do extra jobs after her bike-painting episode a couple of weeks earlier, when she'd managed to cover herself, and all around the house, in green gloss paint.

"Hi, Mum. Hi, sis." Ant parked his bike against the house wall. He dropped his school bag, his high-vis jacket, and cycle helmet, and then sprinted over to see Cinders, their pet rabbit.

"Careful with her. Hold her under the back legs; otherwise, she'll kick," Ant's mum said.

"Hello, Cinders," Ant stroked the rabbit's long grey-flecked ears. He watched as she twitched her nose. "What can you smell?" He put his fingers near her face; she sniffed them before trying to nibble on one.

"Oi, no, they're not carrots, they're my fingers." Ant snatched his hand away; her teeth looked sharp, and he didn't want her to bite him.

Max opened the door to the rabbit run. "Here, Ant, put her back. She has clean water, fresh straw for her bed, and a bunch of lettuce leaves."

"How was school?" His mum asked Ant the usual question.

"Fine, I suppose." Ant gave his usual answer.

"Just fine?" His mum had hoped for more.

"We're doing an end-of-year play ... something about time travel. I've got to read the script to decide who to be."

"I'm sure you can play whoever you want, my little actor." His mum leaned over to give him a hug, and then kissed the top of his head.

"But, we have to sing … it's a musical." Ant looked up at her before wriggling free.

"Sing! I've never heard you sing except for Baa, Baa Black Sheep or Twinkle, Twinkle Little Star, and that was years ago. Knowing you, I'm sure you'll manage to do it; my Ant can do anything." His mum hugged him a second time.

2

"WHAT WILL GRANDAD THINK?"

After leaving Ant, Billy arrived at the back door to his grandad's house; he could see his dog Jacko, and his grandad through the window. He walked straight in.

"Hi, Grandad. Hi, Jacko."

Billy's dog woofed and ran to greet him.

"Oh, Billy, you made me jump. I didn't hear you." Grandad patted his chest to relieve his surprise.

"Are you wearing your hearing aid, Grandad?" Billy shouted.

Grandad put his hand to his ear to check. "Yes, but it's switched off. I don't bother when I'm by myself." He fiddled for a moment. "Say something." Grandad looked to Billy.

"Have you any biscuits in your tin?" Billy held a cheeky grin.

"I heard that ... you are a shocker, young Billy." Grandad reached up to the shelf where he kept the tall round tin with its airtight top, decorated with pictures of different biscuits, including Billy's favourite, custard creams. "Here you are. Only one, mind, or your mother will be after me."

"Thanks, Grandad." Billy took a custard cream. After separating the biscuit in two halves, he set about licking the yellow custard-flavoured filling off.

"Do you want a cup of tea with that?" his Grandad asked.

"Yes, please." Billy resumed licking the biscuit; Jacko pushed his nose toward his hand, hoping to get some. "No, mate, it's not for you." He ruffled the dog's fur.

Billy reached into his school bag, took out a book, and placed it on the kitchen table.

"Careful not to spill tea on your school work," Grandad warned.

"It's not really a school book. Miss gave us a script for our year-end play." Billy turned over the page.

"Have you got a part?" Grandad asked.

"That's what I've got to do tonight. Read the script and decide if I want a part."

"So, what's the play about?" Grandad took his biscuit and dunked it into his tea.

"Time-travel—it's about a teacher who turns into a time traveller and visits famous dates in history like 1066." Billy watched his grandad. "Quick, Grandad, your biscuit will go all soggy."

"Oh blow, I forgot." He lifted the biscuit up just in time to see most of it fall back into the cup with a plop. "Bother, it tastes disgusting like that." Grandad got a spoon and fished around in his tea.

"The play would be fun, but it's a musical, with singing and everything." Billy looked glum as he spoke. "And it lasts for an hour—that's a lot of words and songs to learn. Not like our advert project that we did last term, which lasted a minute."

Grandad scooped out a teaspoon full of brown gunk from his tea and placed it in his saucer. "Here, Jacko," he called.

"No, Grandad, Jacko will get fat if you keep feeding him biscuits." Billy stroked the top of his dog's head. "Sorry, mate, I know you like biscuits, but it's for your own good."

Billy thought he saw Jacko smile. He always loved attention, even though he didn't get the soggy biscuit. His long tail wagged freely.

"You will get your proper food when we get home. Not long now." Billy turned back to reading the script. "The play has five big parts. Ant wants to play the Keymaster; he's the main character."

"What about you? What part do you want to play?" Grandad peered over his shoulder to see the script. "It says here that the main characters are the Keymaster, Samantha, Ben, C-J, and Max."

"As I said, Ant wants to be Keymaster. Samantha is a girl, and I'm definitely not dressing up as a girl. Ben is cheeky, C-J stands for Carla Joe, another girl, and Max is a boy in the play, not like Maxine, Ant's sister. And this Max is sensible and interesting." Billy twisted around to look at his grandad.

"Sensible and interesting. Hardly sounds like you." Grandad shook Billy by the shoulder, "Only joking, lad."

Billy turned a few more pages, reading each of the parts; he shook his head while he studied the book.

"Look, Grandad." Billy pointed at a page. "They all have loads to say and sing." He counted the words of a particularly long speech by the Keymaster. "How will I ever remember? I think I'll just make scenery." He slammed the book shut and flopped back in his seat. Jacko came and stood next to him, resting his head in Billy's lap.

"It's all about practice ... rehearsals," Grandad said, hoping to reassure him.

"But I can't do this." Billy slipped down off his chair and onto the floor to hug Jacko. He buried his face in the dog's fur, not wanting his grandad looking at him.

"Of course, you can. Remember how you behaved nastily to Ant when he won the school prize, and then you realised how you and he are different and good at different things. So, doing what you know you're good at, makes you feel confident."

Grandad flicked through the script, looking for the page that Billy had sat reading. He read the long speech to himself. *Yeah, I'm not sure I could remember that, but I am seventy-five-years-old.* He kept the thought to himself. Instead, he said to Billy, "As I mentioned, it's all about practice, and with your young mind, it shouldn't be a problem ... I tell you what, we can do it together, after school, while you wait for your mum."

"Yeah, but what if I forget my words in front of the whole school and the parents?

I'll look a right idiot."

Grandad's telephone rang. "That will be your mum, I bet. Hello, 824175." He listened before nodding to Billy.

Billy collected up his jacket, helmet, and schoolbag, along with Jacko's lead and collar. Complete with dog, he pulled open the back door. "Thanks, Grandad, see you tomorrow," he said, closing the door as he left.

His mum met Billy at the door to their house. "Why the long face?"

"School," he muttered as he walked in.

"But you like school," she protested. "What's happened today?"

"Oh, nothing, Mum." Billy removed Jacko's lead before heading for the sitting room.

His mum heard the television. "I need your help getting the tea ready," she called after him.

Billy chose not to hear.

She waited for him to reply. "Did you hear me, Billy?" She walked as she spoke. By the time she had finished her sentence, Billy's mum had reached the sitting room. "What about your homework?"

Billy didn't look up; he sat too busy watching the latest Spiderman DVD, for the fifth time at least.

"Come on, Billy, you've seen that loads of times. I need some potatoes and carrots peeling." His mum sounded insistent.

"What are we having?" Billy didn't move his eyes off the TV screen.

"Nothing unless you come and help." His mum bent, picked up the remote control, and hit the *off* button.

"Muuum, I was watching that."

"Come on, Billy, tell me what's wrong."

Billy stood and followed his mum to the kitchen. He shuffled along behind her like an old man rather than a ten-year-old boy.

"It's Miss Tompkins …" he said.

"What? You're not in trouble again?" His mum sure hoped not.

"No, nothing like that. Miss wants to do a year-end play about time travel, and we have to choose the part we want to play."

"That's great. So, why the long face?" She stared.

"Because it's a musical with loads of words and singing, and I know I can't do either." Billy pushed out his bottom lip; it trembled.

3

WHO WILL BE KEYMASTER?

"Okay, year five, you should have read the script for homework last night. Can I have a show of hands from those who want to play the Keymaster." Miss Tompkins looked at the forest of arms. "Well, that's encouraging." She swept her gaze around the classroom, "And I see we have a number of girls wanting to play the role."

"Please, Miss." Julie held up her hand.

"Yes, Julie."

"It doesn't say the Keymaster has to be a boy."

"You're quite right, but with so many of you wanting the part, we'll have to hold auditions."

Ant and Tom leant in; they took no notice of Billy, who just sat staring into space.

"She can't be serious!" Tom had trouble keeping his voice to a whisper. "Half the class wants to be the Keymaster. Just say no girls!" His eyes narrowed while he stared in Julie's direction.

"Girls ought to audition; Julie's right." Ant felt so confident that he would get the part that he didn't mind. He had even started learning the words. Ant noticed that Billy had said nothing. "Hey, what's wrong with you, mate?"

Billy made his hands into fists and

crossed his arms over his chest. "I'll build scenery." His mumble sounded difficult to understand. Dejected, he dropped his head.

Tom and Ant exchanged glances, "What?" They spoke together.

To get the attention of the class, Miss Tompkins wrapped her knuckles on her desk. "For the audition, I want each hopeful to perform the Keymaster part from scene one. I will read the other parts, and the remainder of the class can provide the chorus. So, use the rest of this lesson and break-time to practice."

Scattered around the playground, year five students moved away from everyone else so that they could practice their lines. The curious, mostly juniors, followed them around, mimicking what they did and said, much to the annoyance of the older children.

The sound of the end-of-break bell cleared everybody from the playground as they headed back to class, but for those about to audition, it meant their time was coming, and quickly. The nerves kicked in.

"Hey, Ant, you'll storm it," someone from his class shouted. Ant turned away, it was one thing to feel confident, but something else to actually stand up and act out a part. His stomach made a gurgling sound; he kept walking, not wanting to talk to anyone right now.

While year five had gone to break, Miss had rearranged the classroom, moving the desks and chairs to form a stage area with seating.

"Can I have the first person who wants to audition for the Keymaster?" Miss pointed to the stage. "Come up here, please."

The class fell silent as each person looked at someone else, or the floor, or their script, hoping Miss wouldn't choose them first.

"Well, Julie, it looks like you'll go first."

"But, Miss, I didn't put my hand up," Julie protested.

"I know, but since you seemed so keen to play the Keymaster earlier, I thought …"

"Oh, okay." Julie came and stood in the space that Miss Tompkins had created for the stage. All eyes were fixed on her. She coughed. Just a clearing-of-the-throat sort of cough, but not enough to show how anxious she felt. Her shaking leg told a different story.

"Now, this is your audience." Miss motioned to the rest of the class seated in a semi-circle, "They need to hear and see what you're doing. Hold your script up but not so much that it covers your face. When you feel ready, please begin."

Julie shifted her weight from foot to foot before looking at her script, and then out at the rows of classmates.

"Good morning, class," she squeaked. Her words didn't reach the front row, never mind the whole class.

Miss Tompkins raised her hand to her ear to help her hear. "Julie, you will never fill the assembly hall like that. Draw your breath in; take it right down here." Miss pointed to her stomach. "Then project your voice, nice and loud." Miss did so, as she spoke.

"Good morning, class." Julie's shout echoed around the room, and several of the front row pupils clasped their hands to their ears. Julie looked to Miss.

"Better—" Miss Tompkins said, nodding, "—but no shouting; you just need to project."

Julie continued reading, "I'm your supply teacher for today." She rubbed her hands as she spoke, just as the script instructed. "Right! Battle of Hastings!" she exclaimed.

Miss raised her arm, signalling for Julie to stop, "Now, that sounded a lot better.

We'll pretend you've read the rest of the speech. Turn over the page. Where it says, '*I can go back in time anywhere*', can you sing that line for me, please?" Miss closed her eyes to help her concentrate while she listened to Julie.

Julie broke into what she thought was a song, but her throat, tight with fear, made her sound more like a violin getting played by an angry cat. She squeaked and squawked so much that Miss Tompkins jumped up and snatched the script from her hand.

"Julie ... Julie! That's enough. Thank you. Now, take a seat, please."

Julie slunk off stage, muttering while she walked. "There was no need for that. I didn't say I could sing," she muttered.

"Who's next?" Miss stood and pointed to Khalid. "Will you audition?"

He looked around to check who Miss Tompkins pointed at. "Not for Keymaster, Miss." Khalid had changed his mind; although he liked singing, he thought the part had too many spoken words to learn.

"So, who will?" Miss looked along the rows of seated students. Ant sat smiling back at her. "Come on then, Anthony." She waved him up on stage.

Ant's stomach flipped. He wanted this, but he still felt nervous. In front of the whole class, he stood as tall as he could with his hands behind him; he pushed his chest out and pulled his shoulders back. He wanted to make a good impression.

"Good morning, class!" Ant looked toward Miss, who nodded her approval. "I'm your supply teacher for today." He rubbed his hands like the script said, although he didn't have a script with him. "Right! Battle of Hastings!"

"That was excellent," Miss said. "However, I want to hear you sing now, Anthony. If you turn over the page and start where it says '*I can go back in time …*'." She stopped herself and cocked her head, and her eyebrows met in the middle. "Where's your script?"

"I've learnt the lines off by heart, Miss." Ant checked around the room for his classmates' reaction. His smugness nearly stopped him from singing; he found out that you cannot grin and sing at the same time. Then, putting on a straight face, he sang the whole of the verse.

Miss clapped her hands. "Excellent, Anthony. You've a natural talent."

All the class applauded, except Billy.

In true theatre style, Ant bent at the waist and took a bow, making a full dramatic sweep of his hand like some Shakespearean actor, while urging his classmates to continue clapping.

"That will do; thank you, Anthony. So, who else have we? I counted fifteen hopefuls before break." Miss walked across the stage area, looking at the rows of faces. No one raised their hand. "What happened to all my Keymasters? Tom, your hand went up earlier." Miss held his gaze.

"It's Ant, Miss, he did such a great audition." Tom dropped his eyes.

"Well, unless you try, you'll never know. And you, Suzanna, your project at the end of the last term proved a great success." Miss Tompkins tried to encourage more students.

"I've decided to audition for one of the girl parts. I'm not sure about singing by myself." Suzanna looked to Julie and mouthed, "What do you think?" Julie shrugged.

"Well, if you're sure." Miss sounded disappointed. She cast her eyes over the rest of the rows. Then she noticed Billy, despite the fact he had slipped down in his seat, trying to make himself invisible.

"Come on, Billy." Miss Tompkins had wanted him all along as Keymaster, though she could not say so.

"Do I have to, Miss?" Billy stared at the floor, trying to avoid looking at her directly.

"No, you don't have to, but I think you should, at least, give it ago. Just read a few lines and see how you get on."

"But, Miss, I can't sing for toffee."

"Not sat like that you can't. Billy, come up here and bring your script." Miss Tompkins beckoned to him.

Billy pulled himself into an upright position before standing. "Okay, Miss." The chair legs screeched in protest when he shoved his seat backward. Each stride toward the stage took him an age. Slowly, reluctantly, he made his way forward.

"What do you want me to do?" He knew really but tried anything to delay the moment.

"Hurry up; it'll be lunchtime soon." Miss sounded impatient.

"I can wait, Miss; I don't mind." He turned to head back to his seat.

"No, Billy, now!"

He stopped and held his script so close to his face that no one could see him, and then read as fast as he could. The garbled words barely made it out of his mouth. He turned to head back to his seat.

"You've not sung yet," Miss called him back.

"'Cos I can't sing, Miss." He looked at

her, hoping she might change her mind.

"Just one verse, the three lines from over the page." Miss pointed to the script, "Everyone will sing with you, on the count of three … one … two … three."

Miss led the singing, "I can go back in time, anywhere …" She raised her hand to stop the racket they all made. "Come on, class; there's a lot of room for improvement. Right, again." She raised her arms like an orchestra conductor. "And all together now …"

"I can go back in time, anywhere."

"Keep going."

"I have the keys, the keys to history."

"And finally," she looked at the class over her glasses. Everyone knew they had to try harder.

"Come with me back in time; I'll take you there."

"See, you can do it." She gave the class a clap. "Right, Billy, your turn."

"Oh, Miss." Billy rubbed his hand across his eyes while he tried to think of a reason that he shouldn't.

Miss tapped her foot to the beat of the tune and pointed at Billy to begin.

"I can go back in time, anywhere. I have the keys, the keys to history. Come with me back in time; I'll take you there." Billy's singing sounded more like the croaking of a terrified frog. Finished, he stood without moving, hoping he had done enough to end this nightmare.

"Well, that didn't seem so bad. You won't be in the next boy-band, but that's not why we're here." Miss looked at him, disappointed, and agreed that he wasn't right for the part, but she knew that he could do better.

4

REHEARSALS

The stage in the school hall had been transformed into a modern-day classroom for the opening scene of the Keymaster play. But, as in all theatre productions, it came from an illusion like a magic trick. From where the audience sat, it looked like a classroom, but in reality, the scene builders had made it from several large painted canvases hung from the overhead gallery, plus genuine props like desks and chairs, placed in rows around the stage.

To build a set on stage takes a lot of time

to design, paint, and sort out the props. Miss Tompkins had organised the stage crew from those class members not acting, and since Billy didn't want a part in the play, he became one of her key helpers.

"Stage crew," Miss called out; she could hear someone whistling. "Can I have your attention." The whistling continued. "Who is that?" Miss could not see Billy, as he was working off to one side of the stage with a broad brush and pot of cream-coloured paint, applying it to several screens.

"It's Billy, Miss." Khalid offered. Khalid didn't get a part in the play either and had decided to do scenery instead. He ran off to fetch Billy. "Oi, Field, Miss wants you." He and Billy ambled back to where the rest of the crew waited.

"Nice of you to join us." Miss's sarcasm got lost on Billy.

"Sorry, Miss, I was—"

"That will do, Billy. I just need to tell you all that, as from today, we will no longer have the stage to ourselves. The rehearsals are starting. It means that you need to stay quiet, and especially no whistling." She looked right at Billy, pretending to be cross. In actual fact, she felt pleased that Billy had gotten back to being his old self. He had seemed so glum ever since she had announced the end-of-year performance. "Actors need to hear each other's lines," she said. "So they know when to say theirs. Is that understood?"

"Yes, Miss," they spoke as a group.

Billy stood next to Khalid and brought

his hand up to cover his mouth, "I wonder how Ant's doing as Keymaster?"

"We'll find out soon enough." Khalid pointed toward the main door into the hall as the rest of year five trooped in.

"Actors not only have to learn their lines and songs, but they also need to know when to say them, and where to stand while they say them. Stage rehearsals are necessary for practicing positions, actions, and building confidence," Miss Tompkins explained.

With the whole of year five on stage, she had a large crowd of children gathered around her. Miss Tompkins had trouble making herself heard. "Stage crew, please keep the noise down, and Billy, can you fetch me a piece of chalk." Her shout reached his ears.

Billy disappeared to look for some chalk.

Miss Tompkins raised her voice. "What I'm going to say next is vital. Listen carefully. So that we all move in the correct direction when told to, we need to make sure we know our left from our right." Miss Tompkins held up each of her arms in turn as she spoke. As she peered over her glasses, she didn't feel so sure that this would turn out as easy as it had sounded. "And, in particular, stage left and stage right," She added.

Miss Tompkins paused to gather her thoughts, "Okay, can everyone, including the stage crew, make a line across the front of the stage, facing the audience." She stood back and watched twenty-nine children shuffle about until, eventually, they had sorted themselves out. *It's worse than herding cats,* she thought.

"Now, raise your right ... that's your right arm," Miss Tompkins repeated herself so that no confusion would remain. "And hold it there." She scanned the line and noticed some hesitation. "Tom, since when has your left become your right?"

"'Cos I'm left handed, Miss, and I get confused." Quickly, he switched arms. "How am I supposed to know?"

Miss continued, "In the theatre, knowing your left from your right is particularly useful when taking directions, and for when I say stage left or stage right. Now, put your arms down and turn to your right." A shuffling of feet followed. "You are now facing stage right. Okay?"

The "Yes, Miss" sounded unclear.

Miss Tompkins put her hand to her ear, "I didn't hear that." She moved her glasses down her nose and stared.

"Yes, Miss," came from all the children at once.

"That's better. Now, don't forget it."

"I've found some, Miss." Billy reappeared, waving a stick of white chalk above his head.

"Thank you, Billy." Miss looked at the assembled children. "We need to work out where the Keymaster and others will stand, and which way they will walk on and off stage. That way, no one will crash into each other. ... Now, anyone in the chorus, please move to the back of the stage, toward the left-hand side."

Khalid put up his hand.

"Yes, Khalid."

"Does that include the stage crew, Miss?"

"Yes, I need to see how much room you lot take up." Miss Tompkins looked about for Billy. "Now, Billy, grab your chalk and draw a line around the group and write on it "chorus". C ... h ... o ... r ... u ... s," she spelt it out.

The rest of the rehearsal continued in much the same way until everyone knew his or her positions, and which way they would come on and off stage.

"That's it for today; you can go home

now." Miss Tompkins waved the children away. "Billy, can you stay a minute?" She looked him straight in the eye. "You have been so useful. Would you mind coming to all the after school rehearsals?—If your parents feel okay with that."

"I'll ask, Miss." His eyes widened. "And I'll let you know tomorrow." Billy felt so pleased that she had asked him that he skipped across the stage to catch up with Ant and Tom.

"Guess what?" Billy slapped his mates on the back. "Miss has asked me to stay after school to help out with the rehearsals ... looks like you can't get away from me."

Tom and Ant grinned back at him.

"A bit like a bad smell!" Ant held his nose.

"Yeah, very amusing." Billy kept walking.

Billy's mum agreed to Billy staying for rehearsals, and as the weeks went by, he became familiar with all aspects of the play. He needed to, as Miss Tompkins had him doing the sound effects, organising props, redrawing the marks where the performers stood, and all those things that make a play run smoothly.

As Billy's classmates spoke their words or sang, Billy repeated them in his head. He watched their entrances and exits on stage and noted the action cues. He needed to make sure the right sound effect came at the correct time. Being at all the rehearsals, the words and songs just sort of climbed into his head without him having to think about them. Often, he knew them better than the person saying them. He began to enjoy being part of the production.

5

ANT TRIES TO FLY

Billy pulled up outside Ant's house. He sat astride his bike, using the gatepost for support. Then, looking up at Ant's bedroom, Billy called to him, "Come on, lazy bones." Billy waited to see Ant at the window, or anything to show that he had heard. However, nothing happened.

It was Saturday, so Billy had permission to have his mobile phone. He typed a text. *Quick, down here, now. Tom's down the old quarry woods. We need to get there right away.* He hit the *send* button.

Within a few seconds of him pressing *send,* Ant appeared at his bedroom window, but still in his pyjamas.

"Crikey!" Billy couldn't believe Ant hadn't dressed yet. He shot him off another text. ... *Get down here now. We're missing all the fun!*

Ant disappeared from view, only to reappear a few minutes later coming around the corner of his house, pushing his bike with one hand and stuffing a slice of bread into his mouth with the other. His bike helmet swung below the handlebars while his yellow visibility jacket flapped from his left shoulder. He looked like a one-winged bird as he raced up the garden path.

"What is it?" Ant tried to say, but the

words got lost in a hail of breadcrumbs that spat out as he spoke.

"Yeah, thanks, mate." Billy brushed away the crumbs. "Down the woods, in the old quarry pit. Tom says some of the older boys have built a mega jump. His text says it's awesome; though, I'm not sure you spell awesome "orsum"." Billy looked to Ant for confirmation.

"Yeah, well, Tom's spelling is a little off at times." Ant fastened the chinstrap of his helmet. "Right, let's go." Before he had finished speaking, Ant had set off down the road with Billy racing behind him.

The old quarry pit woods lay only a five-minute ride away at the speed Ant and Billy travelled. As they approached, they heard the shouts of excited youngsters.

"Wow, listen to that lot; sounds like there are loads of kids there." Ant beamed.

At hearing the noise, Ant sensed the excitement, which made him more eager and determined to get there sooner. He pushed on the peddles as hard as he could. The increasing speed added to his eagerness. Ahead, the path disappeared into the woods, hidden by the trees and groups of boys and girls all gawping at the daredevils, who tackled the new bigger jump that the older boys had built. Volleys of shouts went up each time someone plunged over the quarry edge and raced toward the mountain of doom, which sat at the bottom of the steep drop.

"Coming   through!"   Ant   screamed,

ringing his bike's bell for added effect.

Startled, the crowd fumbled and stumbled to get out of his way, as Ant shot past, riding at full speed.

Billy brought up the rear; he made it to the quarry rim just as Ant reached the bottom of the pit before he ascended the jump. Within seconds, Ant had reached the top of the climb. His speed ensured the back wheel followed the front. Both wheels hung in the air, not by an inch or two, but by several feet, and far higher than Ant had ever jumped before.

Billy yanked at his brakes and skidded to a halt. He knew Ant had gotten himself into trouble.

To do a successful jump on a bike takes a lot of practice, and Ant hadn't had any. He had no idea that steering in mid-air isn't a case of twisting the handlebars, but of moving your weight in the direction you want to go. Ant's flightpath took him toward a tree—a large oak that had stood in the same place for hundreds of years.

The cheering of the crowd at Ant's magnificent jump soon turned to shrieks of horror as his bike, followed by him, smashed into the trunk of the oak tree. Both him and his bike tumbled toward the ground.

It seemed like the world had gone into slow motion. No one breathed. Everyone stood, silenced by the drama of Ant lying in a heap.

When Ant struck the ground, the cracking noise could have been mistaken for a branch breaking. It wasn't. Ant's arm had cracked, snapped clean through. As the hospital X-ray later showed, his radius had broken—one of the bones joining his wrist to his elbow.

The pain of the fracture felt intense, and Ant's scream sounded haunting. Everyone gasped together, sounding like a high-speed train disappearing into a tunnel.

Inactivity turned to panic. Billy dropped his bike and jumped down into the quarry pit, running and stumbling as he went. He needed to get to Ant fast.

The crowd followed, and soon, every person had gathered around him. Ant's shrieks had lessened, but his tears had not. He hurt a lot.

Billy bent over him.

"Are you crazy? What the heck happened?" Billy leant in to help his friend.

"Stop!" Dan, one of the older boys, who had learnt first aid in Scouts, pushed his way to the front of the group. "Don't move him." Dan looked around. "Has anyone rung for an ambulance?"

Everyone had their mobile phones out, taking pictures, texting, or calling. The distant sounds of sirens confirmed an ambulance raced its way toward them.

"Hey, mate, you'll be all right." Billy tried to sound reassuring. Ant felt differently. Everything hurt, and he felt drowsy and wanted to be sick.

Billy didn't ride in the ambulance; instead, he got on his bike and dashed around to

Ant's house. He saw Max in the garden. She had Cinders, their rabbit, dressed in a tee shirt taken from her favourite teddy, plus two pink ribbons, one tied around each of the rabbit's ears. Both Cinders and Max squatted on a blanket with cups, plates, teapot, a jug of juice, dandelion leaves, and all sorts of other things ready for a picnic.

"Max, what are you doing? What have you done to Cinders?" Billy's eyes bulged, and his eyebrows shot up into his hair. Surprised to see a dressed rabbit, he had forgotten why he'd gone there.

"We're having a picnic, but Cinders keeps hopping off. Anyway, why shouldn't rabbits wear clothes?" Max asked the question in a normal voice as if it were something someone might say every day.

"Because it's an animal!" Billy held his head in disbelief.

"But she's a girl, and girls like clothes." Max looked past Billy, trying to spot her brother. "I thought you went out with Ant? Where is he?"

"That's why I'm here—he's in hospital." Billy dropped his bike and ran toward the house. "Is your mum in? She needs to come now."

"Yeah." Max scooped up Cinders and ran after Billy. "Why's Ant in hospital?"

"'Cos he crashed into a tree." Billy disappeared through the back doorway. "Mrs Turner? ... Mrs Turner, quick!" His shout found Ant's mum.

"Billy?" She arrived in the kitchen,

"What on Earth's the matter? Why all the shouting? Where's Ant?"

"That's why I'm here, Mrs Turner; he's on his way to hospital! The ambulance took him."

"Ambulance? … Hospital?" Her eyebrows arched. Ant's mum grabbed for her handbag and phone. "Is he all right? Any bones broken? What happened?" She looked about her. "Max, what have you done to Cinders?" She didn't wait for an answer, "Put Cinders back in her cage right now; we need to go." Her voice changed from calm to panic.

Ant's mum stabbed at her phone, "Taxi, taxi." She spoke as she scrolled through her contacts before hitting the *call* key.

"I think I'd better go home, Mrs Turner."

Billy looked at her and waited for a response. When she didn't reply, he edged awkwardly toward the back door. "I'll get my mum to take me to see Ant."

"Yes, sure, see you there." Ant's mum didn't look at him; too busy with her phone. "Yes, okay." She waved, dismissively, in Billy's direction. "Oh, hello, can I have a taxi …"

6

NO KEYMASTER

"Morning, children." Miss Tompkins cast her eyes down; not her usual cheerful self. "I'm sure you have all heard about Anthony Turner's accident over the weekend." All the class nodded together. "I spoke to his mother, and she assures me he'll make a full recovery."

The children all started to clap and chat at once, speculating about what had happened to Ant.

"Okay, that will do. Now, can we have some quiet." Miss slid her spectacles down her nose and peered over the top. A hand went up. "Yes, Julie."

"Do you know what Ant did, Miss? Everybody says he tried to fly." Julie looked around at her class. All the children laughed.

Miss Tompkins looked directly at Billy and Tom. "Were you two there?"

"Yes, Miss," Billy said; Tom nodded also.

"And?"

"Ant didn't try to fly but wanted to do a jump on his bike, and sort of got it wrong. Instead of landing, he crashed into a tree and broke an arm and ribs," Billy said.

"So, there you have it, children, and now everyone knows. But we do have a problem. It's Monday, and our big performance is on Thursday. And, according to Anthony's mother, he won't be well enough by then." Miss looked despondent.

"But, Miss, no Ant, no Keymaster!" Julie said. Mutters and murmurings followed as her classmates realised what 'no Ant' meant.

"That's the problem, Julie. I know you've all worked so hard, but without the Keymaster, the performance will have to get cancelled."

"Oh, Miss, no. That's not fair." The noise in the classroom reached new heights.

"Children!" Miss Tompkins slapped her hand on the desk repeatedly, hitting it harder with each strike. "Children, quiet, now! I know it feels disappointing, but unless we have a new Keymaster, there is nothing we can do. So, for the rest of the day and this evening, we will all think about the problem and see if we can come up with an answer."

Billy sat astride his bike, waiting for Tom. As Ant wasn't at school, Billy rode part of the way home with Tom.

"That's really poo," Tom said as he pulled alongside Billy.

"Maybe Miss or another teacher can read the part of Keymaster," Billy suggested.

"Yeah, but it won't be the same. We need another kid to do it. Perhaps someone from year six or—" Tom hesitated. "—what about you?" He tried to catch Billy's eye as he spoke. Billy kept looking forward; he didn't answer. They rode in silence.

The boys reached the point where they went their separate ways. "Think about it," Tom shouted over his shoulder as he headed off in a different direction. "Think about it."

Though the distance between the boys had grown, Billy heard him loud and clear. His stomach cramped. *I can't do it; there's not enough time, I can't sing, and I don't want to look stupid.* The thoughts raced through his head.

Billy pulled into his grandad's garden and let himself in the back door as usual. Jacko greeted him.

"Hi, Grandad." Billy bent to pat his dog. "How are you, boy?" Billy gave the dog a tight hug. He hoped Jacko would distract him from thinking about what Tom had suggested. Jacko's tail swished back and forth. Then, after struggling, the dog broke free and ran off, only to reappear seconds later with a rubber bone in his mouth. He dropped it in front of Billy.

"Sorry, boy; I need to talk to Grandad."

"Here we are." Grandad passed Billy a mug of tea. "Just how you like it, and ..." Grandad waved the biscuit tin in front of Billy. "I bought some more of your favourites."

Billy took two custard creams.

His grandad stared at him. "Two! What will your mum say?"

"We've had some bad news at school." Billy licked at the creamy yellow biscuit filling.

"Oh, I'm sorry to hear that." Grandad replaced his cheery smile with a more serious look, "Nothing too bad, I hope."

"It's Ant … well, not actually Ant, but 'cos of his accident, he won't get better before Thursday."

Grandad's brow furrowed.

Billy said, "Remember, the day of our school performance. The one you're coming to with Mum. Well, you were, but with no Ant, we have no Keymaster." Billy bit into his biscuit with a loud crunch. "So, Miss will have to cancel."

"What? After all that hard work, rehearsals, scenery painting, costume making …" Grandad took a drink of his tea. "Surely, the school can do something."

"Miss is looking for a new Keymaster,

but if she can't find one by tomorrow, it'll definitely get cancelled."

Billy and Grandad fell silent, thinking about the situation. The only noise came from the crunching of biscuit, and the disgruntled snuffling from under the table, as Jacko made it clear he wanted to play.

Billy looked up at the kitchen clock, hoping his mum would telephone soon. He needed to go home. Tom's words still played havoc in his head, and if his grandad came to the same conclusion as Tom, he would find it difficult to say no. His gut tightened at the idea.

After a few minutes, Grandad broke the silence, "I know—" he said. "Each evening that you've come back from rehearsals, you always sing or recite words. You must know them all by now."

Oh, no, here it comes. A surge of electricity shot down Billy's spine, and his mouth went dry.

"Why don't you play this Keymaster chap? That'll solve everyone's problems." Grandad peered into Billy's eyes.

Billy put his hands to his face, trying to avoid making eye contact. "Because I can't do it," he mumbled.

Grandad reached out and, with a gentle tug, pulled Billy's arms aside. "What do you mean, you can't do it? How do you know unless you try? If you don't at least have a go, then everyone will feel disappointed. But if you do, you'll save the day. It doesn't matter how well you do, as everyone will be on your side and wish you on."

"Suppose so." Billy sounded unsure.

"You will become the hero, just like that spider chap you keep watching." Grandad beamed a big smile.

"Spiderman," Billy muttered.

"Yes, him. I know, why don't you pretend you're him and use your superpowers to help you get through the performance?" Grandad put his arm around Billy's shoulders. "I'll help you practice. In fact, better than that, why don't we go around to Ant's house right now and talk to him?"

Outside the front door to Ant's house, Grandad stood next to Billy. He rested his arm on Billy's shoulders and held him tight so that he felt supported. Grandad took up the doorknocker. "Are you ready for this?" Billy shuddered at the question. Grandad gave him a reassuring squeeze.

"Yes." Billy nodded.

Grandad rapped the knocker several times. It seemed to takes ages for someone to reach the door.

"They're not in." Billy turned on his heels.

Grandad maintained his grip on Billy's shoulder. "Just give it a little longer." Grandad smiled down at him.

"Who is it?" Max called from the far side of the closed door. "Mummy said we don't want any."

"It's me," Billy said when he recognised Max's voice. "We've come to see Ant."

The front door opened slowly, and

Max's head came into view. "Why didn't you say so?" She shifted her gaze. "Oh, hi, Billy's granddad." Max swung the door fully open, "Mum's in Ant's bedroom. You should see him, all puffy-eyed with blueyyellowish coloured bruising down one side. His arm's in a sling thing, all stiff and white. He even let me write on it in red marker pen. Come on; I'll show you." Max walked as she talked, leading Billy and Grandad upstairs. "Muuuum, Billy's here!" Max pushed open the bedroom door.

"Flipping heck, mate!" Any fear Billy had about playing the Keymaster disappeared in an instant. "You look awful." The words escaped before Billy could stop them.

Ant tried to say, "So would you if you

rammed your face into a tree," but it came out more like a series of grunts as if his mouth was stuffed with cotton wool. His face looked like a balloon. All swollen with two slits where his eyes should have been.

"You won't get better by Thursday." Billy stated the obvious. "Miss knows; she's talking about cancelling the performance unless someone else plays Keymaster."

Ant dropped his head. "It's not fair." He raised his broken arm. "I can't do nothing with this."

"Oh come on, cheer up; it's not half as bad as it looks." Ant's mum plumped up his pillows to make him more comfortable. "Maybe Miss Tompkins will put it off until next term. He's so looking forward to acting the part."

Billy flashed a look at his grandad, "But, I'll play ..." Billy realised how important playing the part was to Ant and stopped himself.

Ant's mum passed Ant a beaker of juice with a straw. "He's talked about nothing else, my little star." She ruffled his hair.

"You know Jackie's leaving school," Max said. "Her dad got a job somewhere. Her sister's in my class. She told me."

"Yeah, but she can't, she's C-J. If she's not here next term ..." Billy thought for a bit, "It has to get done on Thursday." Billy's eyes darted between Ant, Ant's mum, and his grandad. The time had come to be a superhero. Billy stood as tall as he could and took a large gulp of air. In his deepest grown-up voice, he announced,

"I'll tell Miss that I'll play the Keymaster."
Spiderman would know what to do, he
thought.

Upon hearing Billy, Ant choked on his
juice and coughed so hard that he sprayed
it all over his duvet cover.

"I know I won't do it as well as you."
Billy stood by Ant's side, patting his back
as if burping a baby. "But everyone has
worked so hard, and if Jackie does move
away ..." He stopped talking, waiting for
Ant to breathe normally. "Would you feel
okay if I do it?"

"Well, I can't." Ant's shoulders slumped;
he swallowed hard with the
disappointment. "I guess if anyone other
than me should play the Keymaster, then
Billy's it." Ant turned toward his mum,

"Can you take me to see him? A laugh will help me get better much quicker." As much as Ant wanted to smile, his swollen face stopped him, and instead, his cheeks puffed up even larger like an over-excited hamster.

7

BILLY SAVES THE DAY

Mrs Johnston, the head teacher of Grove Road primary school, stood on stage to talk to the whole school during morning assembly.

"It is with great regret that I have to announce …" Mrs Johnston looked over at Miss Tompkins, who tilted her head in confirmation. "That the year five production of the Keymaster play, due to take place on Thursday afternoon …"

Before she could finish, Billy guessed what she was about to say and jumped to his feet and ran toward the stage. "Will take place!" His shout came out louder than intended, but he managed to stop the announcement. In a single leap, Billy bounded up the stairs and onto the stage and arrived alongside a rather curious head teacher.

"What do you mean? Miss Tompkins told me that the play had to get cancelled because Anthony Turner has broken his arm."

"He has, Mrs Johnston, and his face got all smashed up, but we have a new Keymaster." Billy beamed out at the rows of children.

Mrs Johnston creased her brow while raising one eyebrow. She looked, first, at Billy, then at Miss Tompkins, who just shrugged, then back at Billy.

"Who is this person?" Mrs Johnston bent and gazed into Billy's face. "Explain yourself."

Every pupil and staff member leant in and stared at Billy. Suddenly, he felt deeply self-conscious, and his leg wobbled.

"I didn't have time to tell Miss Tompkins."

"Well, tell us all, now." Mrs Johnston swept her arm out in the direction of the waiting faces.

Billy sensed the anticipation; he had a bout of nerves. "It's me." He said it so quietly that no one heard. *Come on, Spiderman; you can do it.*

"Pardon." Mrs Johnston spoke while several calls from his classmates rang out,

"Oi, Field; speak up. We can't hear anything."

Billy took a deep breath, "It's me." He spoke with great projection, and his voice filled the entire hall.

"You?" Miss Tompkins couldn't hide her relief or surprise. "Well, Billy, that's fantastic." Miss Tompkins focused her gaze on the back of the hall where her year five class sat celebrating. She raised two thumbs, "Full dress rehearsal today," she called to them, as she walked over to where Billy stood. "So, why have you decided to play the part?"

"Because my grandad said that if you don't try, you won't know. And, anyway, 'cos I've been at all the rehearsals, I know the words and songs for the Keymaster and everything." Billy jumped off the stage and raced off to join his classmates.

Tom and Khalid gathered around. "Will you really do it?"

"Me, the superhero ..." Billy sped down the corridor, bent forward with his right arm stretched out in front and his left trailing behind, pretending he could move like Spiderman. "Just watch me," he called back over his shoulder.

Billy's mum, Patti, walked into Grandad's house. Jacko pulled on his lead; going to Grandad's meant sneaked treats.

"Jacko, no." She held his lead tight. "Are you ready?" Patti called out.

Grandad appeared in the kitchen, dressed in a grey flat-cap, long dark-grey overcoat, and black leather gloves. Around his neck, he wore his paisley patterned scarf that Billy had given him for his birthday. To complete his outfit, he had on his black, highly polished leather shoes, which reminded him of when he used to be in the army.

"Come on, we need to collect Ant and his mum. I promised them a lift to school." Billy's mum tapped at her watch. "It starts in half an hour."

Grandad, Patti, and Jacko set off for Ant's house. "Don't be surprised when you see Ant; he's had a nasty fall, which has left him quite bruised," Grandad warned before he clattered the front doorknocker.

Ant's mum opened the door. "It's so kind of you, Patti. I didn't fancy getting a taxi to school, not with Ant looking like he does. He's nearly ready; come in for a minute. It's difficult getting him dressed with his plaster cast and all the swelling. It hurts if you touch him too." She disappeared upstairs.

All three waited in the hallway, listening to a stream of cries—ouch; no, Mum; oi, careful—as Ant's dressing progressed. Eventually, he and his mum appeared at the top of the stairs.

Ant looked more like a snowman, similar in shape but not white. Instead, he appeared various shades of dark blue and black—both his outfit and any skin visible. His head remained swollen, and the only hat that nearly fitted him was his dad's fishing hat, and even so, its brim rested just above his nose. He also had several jumpers covering the miles of bandage he had wrapped around his chest to support his cracked ribs. Over the jumpers, he wore a dark-blue puffer jacket with an inner lining. Both zipped to the top, which made their collars stand up, completely covering his chin and touching the underside of his nose.

His bottom half looked quite normal — just a pair of blue jeans — until his legs came into view. Because his feet had gotten cut and bruised, he couldn't wear shoes. Instead, he wore slippers — deep-red, oversized, and thickly-padded Angry Birds with yellow beaks that wobbled as he walked.

When he descended the stairs, his eyes

became visible; still puffy but now turning yellow. He looked like a chameleon. Not wanting to get laughed at by his school friends, he had borrowed his mum's designer sunglasses that she'd bought off the internet. He slipped them on.

"Okay, all ready." Ant's mum sounded jolly and, seemingly, unaware of Ant's concern.

"Great ... well, we'd better get going." Patti looked Ant up and down but managed to hide her surprise.

Grandad noticed, but as he had no idea about fashion, he just thought Ant was trendy. Jacko only had an interest in protecting everyone from the Angry Birds slippers and barked every time Ant took a step.

SUPERPOWERS RULE

The stage curtains remained closed. From behind them, the assembled cast of children could hear their audience arriving and settling. The general level of excitement felt infectious, and everyone chatted about how year five's performance would go, following the swap-out of the main character only two days earlier. Billy, too, wondered the exact same thing. He had rehearsed his lines in his head so much that he felt confused.

"Come on." Billy noticed that the wall

clock pointed to one-fifty-five. "Still five minutes to starting." The waiting seemed the worst part.

No one heard his comments; lost in the roar of laughter, cheers, and catcalls coming from the audience.

On stage, nobody knew what had caused the outburst, but Ant did.

Miss Tompkins had saved four seats in the front row for Ant, his mum, and Billy's mum and grandad. Jacko would have to sit on the floor. As they walked the length of the hall, everyone got a good look at them, and in particular, Ant. Still dressed the same as when he'd left home, he didn't receive sympathy or care but, instead, finger pointing, peals of laughter, and name-calling. His oversized hat, sunglasses, and zipped-up clothing hid his embarrassment.

Miss Tompkins walked on stage in front of the closed curtains.

"Good afternoon." The noise in the hall remained the same. "Children and parents," she tried again. "Welcome to our year five end-of-term play." She slid her glasses down her nose.

A chorus of "Shush" went up as children noticed. Miss Tompkins had become well known for staring over her glasses.

"Thank you," Miss Tompkins said. "Today, we have a remarkable play for your enjoyment. Remarkable because, on Monday, I was about to cancel the performance following an unfortunate accident involving Anthony Turner who was to play the main character. However, the good news is that Anthony will make a full recovery, and has joined us here today." Miss pointed at Ant. More cheers and catcalls followed. "Quiet, now. And Billy Field volunteered to take on the part with only two days" notice." Miss led the clapping. As she did, she backed off stage, the lights in the hall dimmed, and the stage curtains slid back.

"Good morning, class," Billy delivered the opening line. His voice filled the hall, but in his stomach, a thousand butterflies took flight. Think Superman, he told himself.

In response, the other children delivered

the next line, "Morning, sir …"

"I'm your supply teacher for today," Billy continued in character, and he even remembered to rub his hands together as the script stated. "Right! Battle of Hastings!" Having spoken his line, Billy stood silent and waited. The rest of the cast waited. Everyone in the hall waited.

Soon, mutterings could be heard from the chorus—"Where's the music?"… "We need the music."… "Who's turning on the music?"

At the side of the stage, Miss Tompkins stood flapping her arms like sails in a gale-force wind.

"She wants you, Billy," someone said in a whisper loud enough for the whole audience to hear.

"Not now; I'm acting ..." Beads of sweat broke out on Billy's forehead.

Miss Tompkins still waved frantically. During all the rehearsals, he had taken responsibility for the music and lights, and no one else knew what to do.

Okay, Spiderman, it's down to you. Billy bent forward and, leading with his right arm, he leapt off the stage, ran to the back of the hall, up the stairs, and into the sound and lighting control room. There, he pressed the *on* button for the CD player, and then raced back to take up his position on stage.

The music burst through the speakers just as Billy made it back in time to sing his lines. Nobody heard him sing as the applause drowned out his efforts.

The rest of the play continued without major incident. Khalid took over responsibility for sounds and lights, and apart from a few missed cues, which no one noticed that much, he did all right.

With the final curtain, Miss Tompkins came on stage.

"Well done, year five. Everyone did so well, but I have to congratulate Billy Field for stepping in at such short notice. I know Anthony would have made a splendid Keymaster—as I saw from rehearsals—but Billy really did save the day." Miss gestured to Billy to join her. "Let's hear it for Billy Field."

The whole audience stood. Everyone clapped their hardest, and those that could, whistled, or called out *bravo* or *well done*. The noise in the hall reached a new height. Billy stood fixed to the spot with all the admiration he received.

Patti, Billy's mum, dropped Jacko's lead while she clapped. The dog took the opportunity to dash onto the stage and sit next to his master. Seated on his haunches, Jacko held his head high as if to say, *I'm proud of you, too.*

Later, back at Ant's house, his mum produced tea and cake for everyone.

Billy felt as if he were flying. All the excitement of the performance, and the cheers and good wishes, gave him a real buzz. He liked the feeling, and felt so pleased that he had done it.

"You know, Ant, it was a good thing you smashed into the tree. It meant I had to do something that I didn't want to do. My grandad's right; if you don't try, you'll never know."

Ant had just taken a bite of cake. "What?" A spray of sponge cake covered the table. "Look at me. I'm like a Weeble, and it hurts loads, and I missed my big chance to act in front of the whole school." Ant couldn't speak more for coughing.

"Yeah, and I'm sorry that something bad had to happen to you for me to realise that I could do something I didn't think I could. Now, I feel proud of myself. And I'm sorry that you missed your chance to act, but you already knew you were a good actor. If I hadn't given it a go, I would never have dared to do it."

Ant's eyes watered from the coughing.

Billy said, "You're a real mate, Ant, and as soon as you feel better, I'll do something special for you to show how much I like being your best friend."

Gently, Billy slapped Ant's back. The remainder of the cake had gone down the wrong way. "Come on mate; cough it up."

THE END

WHAT YOU CAN LEARN FROM 'BILLY SAVES THE DAY.'

Confidence is a feeling linked strongly to self-esteem. It is the belief in ourselves that we can do something well, and succeed at it. It is the value that we put on ourselves, and how we perceive ourselves to be. For most people, their self-esteem changes both with age and with events and experiences that happen in their lives. For example, confidence can start low before you learn a new skill, but then rise as you become more competent, or it can rise dramatically if you get complemented or encouraged. What we need to be aware of is that if we tell ourselves and believe that we can't do something or we're not good at something, then that's what happens. We can't, and we're not!

Children have to experience difficult situations to learn for themselves who they are. They go through the feelings of self-doubt, guilt, fear, and anxieties, but it's the meaning they put on the feelings from about the age of seven that impacts who they become—and how they form their identity. If a child has not been loved and nurtured, they are likely to believe themselves unworthy of love, or not likable, or at worst, simply a bad person. However, a child that has received encouragement, support, proper boundaries, and unconditional love will believe that they are lovable, worthy, safe, and capable.

Self-belief and self-esteem are internal feelings and, therefore, not parts of a person that can be seen. It's like an iceberg where what you see is just above the surface. Deep below lies the truth of how people actually feel. It's a part that they don't show to the outside world and, sometimes, not even to themselves. When we don't understand why we feel the way we do, why we feel that we are not good enough or not lovable enough, the reason can get hidden deep beneath the waters.

In the story, Billy is given an opportunity to act in the school play, but he tells himself he can't do it. He convinces himself that he'll never learn and remember all the lines. He feels so unsure of himself and vulnerable that he begins to think of all the ways he can get out of playing a part. But he is capable and, without even realising it, he learns the lines, not only for the main part but all the other parts too. When he finds that he has no option but to save the day and play the main part, he realises that he is able and sees that he can believe in his abilities.

At times like this, we have to dig deep into those waters to find evidence that what we've told ourselves may not be true. The best way to do this is to think of another time when we felt secure, proud of ourselves, able, and confident. Or to take on the persona of someone we admire, like Spiderman in the story. When we feel the positive feelings that this brings, we can approach what we might anticipate as a negative task with a different thought, a different attitude, and we find that we can do anything we put our minds to. We just need to believe we can and, guess what, we can!

It is not the mountain we conquer but ourselves.
Sir Edmund Hillary

If you're presenting yourself with confidence, you can pull off pretty much anything.
Katy Perry

GET YOUR FREE ACTIVITY BOOK

To accompany all the Billy books there is a free **activity book** for each title. Each activity book includes word search, crossword, secret message, maze and cryptogram puzzles plus pictures to colour.

To get your **free** Activity Book go to **www.thebillybooks.co.uk** and click the button **Get Your Free Activity Book**. Then click the cover of the book matching this book

BOOK REVIEW

If you found this book helpful, leaving a review on Goodreads.com or other book related websites would be much appreciated by me and others who have yet to find it.

READ ON FOR A TASTER OF

BILLY WANTS IT ALL

BILLY GROWING UP SERIES: VALUE OF MONEY

James Minter

Helen Rushworth – Illustrator

www.billygrowingup.com

AT THE

SUPERMARKET

"Oh, Mum, do I have to?" Billy slumped down in the back seat of the car and clicked the seatbelt into place. "It's not fair! Why do I always have to go to the supermarket?" He stared hard at the back of his mum's head as she drove. He hoped she might turn into an alien or something. *Anything* rather than go shopping.

"Funny, you didn't say that when we went to London looking for that new skateboard shop." His mum watched him in the rear-view mirror.

Billy noticed and snarled back at her, "Yeah, well ... that's different."

"I'll tell you what, you stop eating, or wearing clothes, or going to the toilet, or having a shower, or cleaning your teeth, or any of the other things you do, like having clean sheets on your bed, shoes on your feet, and Jacko as a pet, then you won't need to come shopping. How does that sound?"

"Muuum, be serious. All I'm saying is why do I have to go shopping?" Billy gazed out of the car window; they passed the park. "Look! See, it's Tom, Ant, and

Khalid." He tapped his finger hard against the glass, trying to get her attention. "Please, Mum, stop and let me out."

"I know that Lindy takes Ant and Max when she goes shopping, so why shouldn't you come with me?" Billy's mum slowed the car as they approached a pedestrian crossing. The lights had turned red. By chance, Lindy and Max stood on the crossing.

"See!" Billy screeched, "Ant's not with them." He crossed his arms over his chest and jabbed his fists deep into his armpits while pushing his chin forward.

"You can sulk all you like, but you will help me with the shopping."

Billy took a trolley and scooted across the car park, following his mum into the supermarket. As they wandered up and down each aisle, working their way through a long list of items, every now and then, Billy's hand would shoot out. He waited until his mum got distracted reading a label or trying to work out how many ounces in a gram, and then he would grab a packet of sweets or biscuits or shower gel in a Spiderman-shaped bottle, or anything else that took his fancy.

"No, Billy! How many more times?" His mum reached into the trolley and put each item back, placing them randomly on shelves that contained something totally unrelated but which they happened to be passing at the time. "You know money doesn't grow on trees." His mum narrowed her eyes and glared at him. "And anyway, too much sugar is bad for you."

"Yeah, but what about the Spiderman gel? You want me to be nice and clean, don't you?"

"Did you see the price of it compared to the supermarket's brand? It's twice as much." His mum held his gaze.

"I suppose so." Billy dropped his head. As he did, he spotted one of those dental chew dog bones. "What about this?" Billy grabbed the packet. "If you get this for Jacko, you won't have to pay for a dog dentist." Proudly, he waved the bone in his mum's face.

"Now, that makes sense. Investing in this dog chew today could mean we'll save on vet bills in the future." She took the packet from Billy and dropped it into the trolley.

Billy screwed up his eyes and creased his brow, "In whating?"

"Investing. ... It's when you make money work for you." His mum reached into the trolley and took up the chew bone again. "See here; it's four pounds and eighty pence." She held it out for Billy to see. "But the last time we got Jacko's teeth cleaned by the vet it cost over two hundred and seventy pounds."

"Crikey, that's nearly the cost of two skateboards. The one I want is only one hundred and forty pounds." Billy took the bone back. "Does that mean if we buy this, you can buy me my skateboard with the money saved?" He tilted his head to one side and made a cheesy grin. "Please," he added, for good measure.

His mum pretended not to hear as she loaded more items into the trolley. "Pick up that sack of potatoes for me, please, and then we're finished."

Billy squatted and lifted the sack. He let out a grunt as he strained. "Well?" he asked again.

His mum still didn't answer. "A growing boy like you should be able to lift that."

Billy staggered, lifting the sack high enough to push it over the side of the trolley. It dropped onto all the other shopping.

"Careful, or you'll crush everything." Billy's mum manoeuvred the sack to one side. "Right, let's go and pay."

The car boot shut with a loud thud. "Okay, good job. Time to get this lot home." Billy's mum slipped into the driver's seat.

On the far side of the car park, Billy saw some teenagers practicing with their skateboards.

"Look, Mum, see that boy there?" Billy pushed his arm between the car's front seats and pointed, "The one in the blue jacket. He's got the board I want—an Element Nyjah Weaver. I saw it in the *Boards and Bikes* catalogue."

"But you've got a skateboard, the one you bought from Dan Prescott with your birthday money. What's wrong with that?" Billy's mum drove on, leaving Billy hanging over the back seat and watching his dream board disappear into the distance.

"It's okay, but I'm getting really good. Even Stu says so."

"Stu … Stewart Dunderdale? I told you to keep away from him." Billy's mum frowned.

Billy didn't see, as he still sat looking out of the back window, but he heard his mum's disapproval.

"Yeah, but he reckons I ought to go in for the under-fifteens competition."

"But you're only ten." His mum sounded hesitant, "Are you sure he said fifteen?"

"Yeah, 'cos that's how good I am." Billy's smile couldn't have been wider when he thought about what Stu had said. "So, can I?"

"How's your friend Ant getting on? Is he as good as you?" Billy's mum stopped the car outside their house.

"He's learning slowly, but he's nervous after breaking his arm where he smashed into that tree on his bike."

"I'm sure he is. Are you helping him to improve his skateboarding?"

"Not really; I let him use my board sometimes, but he can't even drop or pump or do a kick turn." Billy sounded very matter of fact, but his mum didn't have a clue as to what he was talking about.

"Oh, that's a shame. Maybe you can teach him." His mum rubbed her chin while she thought. "You say Stu says you're good enough to go in for the under-fifteens competition. Does that mean there are lots of children who aren't that good compared to you?"

"I guess so." Billy had the sack of potatoes over his shoulder as he strode up the garden path. "Where do you want these?"

"What about giving lessons? If you're that good, you can offer to teach other children and charge them. Then your skateboard is an investment, as you can earn money from it and put it toward that elephant hinge thingy board you want."

"Oh, Mum, it's called an Element Nyjah Weaver."

I HOPE YOU ENJOYED THIS FREE CHAPTER. READ 'BILLY WANTS IT ALL" TO FIND OUT WHAT HAPPENS NEXT...

FOR PARENTS, TEACHERS, AND GUARDIANS: ABOUT THE 'BILLY GROWING UP" SERIES

Billy and his friends are children entering young adulthood, trying to make sense of the world around them. Like all children, they are confronted by a complex, diverse, fast-changing, exciting world full of opportunities, contradictions, and dangers through which they must navigate on their way to becoming responsible adults.

What underlies their journey are the values they gain through their experiences. In early childhood, children acquire their values by watching the behaviour of their parents. From around eight years old onwards, children are driven by exploration, and seeking independence; they are more outward looking. It is at this age they begin to think for themselves, and are capable of putting their own meaning to feelings, and the events and experiences they live through. They are developing their own identity.

The Billy Books series supports an initiative championing Values-based Education, (VbE) founded by Dr Neil Hawkes*. The VbE objective is to influence a child's capacity to succeed in life by encouraging them to adopt positive values that will serve them during their early lives, and sustain them throughout their adulthood. Building on the VbE objective, each Billy book uses the power of traditional storytelling to contrast negative behaviours with positive outcomes to illustrate, guide, and shape a child's understanding of the importance of values.

This series of books help parents, guardians and teachers to deal with the issues that challenge children who are coming of age. Dealt with in a gentle way through storytelling, children begin to understand the challenges they face, and the importance of introducing positive values into their everyday lives. Setting the issues in a meaningful context helps a child to see things from a different perspective. These books act as icebreakers, allowing easier communication between parents, or other significant adults, and children when it comes to discussing difficult subjects. They are suitable for KS2, PSHE classes.

There are eight books are in the series. Suggestions for other topics to be dealt with in this way are always welcome. To this end, contact the author by email: james@jamesminter.com.

*Values-Based Education, (VbE) is a programme that is being adopted in schools to inspire adults and pupils to embrace and live positive human values. In English schools, there is now a Government requirement to teach British values. More information can be found at: www.valuesbasededucation.com/

BILLY GETS BULLIED

Bullies appear confident and strong. That is why they are scary and intimidating. Billy loses his birthday present, a twenty-pound note, to the school bully. With the help of a grown-up, he manages to get it back and the bully gets what he deserves.

BILLY AND ANT FALL OUT

False pride can make you feel so important that you would rather do something wrong than admit you have made a mistake. In this story, Billy says something nasty to Ant and they row. Ant goes away and makes a new friend, leaving Billy feeling angry and abandoned. His pride will not let him apologise to his best friend until things get out of hand.

BILLY IS NASTY TO ANT

Jealousy only really hurts the person who feels it. It is useful to help children accept other people's successes without them feeling vulnerable. When Ant wins a school prize, Billy can't stop himself saying horrible things. Rather than being pleased for Ant, he is envious and wishes he had won instead.

BILLY AND ANT LIE

Lying is very common. It's wrong, but it's common. Lies are told for a number of different reasons, but one of the most frequent is to avoid trouble. While cycling to school, Billy and Ant mess around and lie about getting a flat tyre to cover up their lateness. The arrival of the police at school regarding a serious crime committed earlier that day means their lie puts them in a very difficult position.

BILLY HELPS MAX

Stealing is taking something without permission or payment. Children may steal for a dare, or because they want something and have no money, or as a way of getting attention. Stealing shows a lack of self-control. Max sees some go-faster stripes for her bike. She has to have them, but her birthday is ages away. She eventually gives in to temptation.

BILLY SAVES THE DAY

Children need belief in themselves and their abilities, but having an inflated ego can be detrimental. Lack of self-belief holds them back, but overpraising leads to unrealistic expectations. Billy fails to audition for the lead role in the school play, as he is convinced he is not good enough.

BILLY WANTS IT ALL

The value of money is one of the most important subjects for children to learn and carry with them into adulthood, yet it is one of the least-taught subjects. Billy and Ant want skateboards, but soon realise a reasonable one will cost a significant amount of money. How will they get the amount they need?

BILLY KNOWS A SECRET

You keep secrets for a reason. It is usually to protect yourself or someone else. This story explores the issues of secret-keeping by Billy and Ant, and the consequences that arise. For children, the importance of finding a responsible adult with whom they can confide and share their concerns is a significant life lesson.

MULTIPLE FORMATS

Each of the Billy books is available as a **paperback**, as a **hardback** including coloured pictures, as **eBooks** and in **audio**-book format.

COLOURING BOOK

The Billy Colouring book is perfect for any budding artist to express themselves with fun and inspiring designs. Based on the Billy Series, it is filled with fan-favourite characters and has something for every Billy, Ant, Max and Jacko fan.

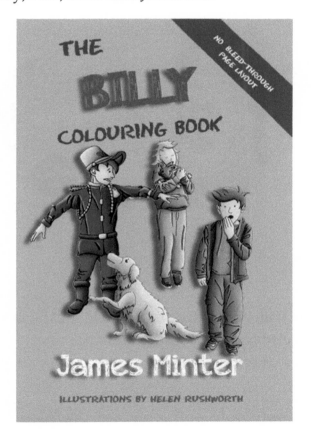

THE BILLY BOOKS COLLECTIONS
VOLUMES 1 AND 2

For those readers who cannot wait for the next book in the series, books 1, 2, 3, and 4 are combined into a single work — The Billy Collection, Volume 1, whilst books 5, 6, 7, and 8 make up Volume 2.

The collections are still eligible for the free activity books. Find them all at www.thebillybooks.co.uk .

ABOUT THE AUTHOR

I am a dad of two grown children and a stepfather to three more. I started writing five years ago with books designed to appeal to the inner child in adults - very English humour. My daughter Louise, reminded me of the bedtime stories I told her and suggested I write them down for others to enjoy. I haven't yet, but instead, I wrote this eight-book series for 7 to 9-year-old boys and girls. They are traditional stories dealing with negative behaviours with positive outcomes.

Although the main characters, Billy and his friends, are made up, Billy's dog, Jacko, is based on our much-loved family pet, which, with our second dog Malibu, caused havoc and mayhem to the delight of my children and consternation of me.

Prior to writing, I was a college lecturer and later worked in the computer industry, at a time before smartphones and tablets, when computers were powered by steam and stood as high as a bus.

WEBSITES

www.billygrowingup.com

www.thebillybooks.co.uk

www.jamesminter.com

E-MAIL

james@jamesminter.com

TWITTER

@james_minter

@thebillybooks

FACEBOOK

facebook.com/thebillybooks/

facebook.com/author.james.minter

ACKNOWLEDGEMENTS

Like all projects of this type, there are always a number of indispensable people who help bring it to completion. They include Christina Lepre, for her editing and incisive comments, suggestions and corrections. Harmony Kent for her proofreading, and Helen Rushworth of Ibex Illustrations, for her images that so capture the mood of the story. Gwen Gades for her cover design. And Maggie, my wife, for putting up with my endless pestering to read, comment and discuss my story, and, through her work as a personal development coach, her editorial input into the learnings designed to help children become responsible adults.

IBEX ILLUSTRATIONS

9 781910 727218